The Quahog Stops Here

Other Books

by

Don Bousquet

BEWARE OF THE QUAHOG

THE QUAHOG WALKS AMONG US

I BRAKE FOR QUAHOGS

THE NEW ENGLAND EXPERIENCE

THE BEST OF THE QUAHOG TRILOGY

DON BOUSQUET'S NEW ENGLAND

Don Bousquet

The Quahog Stops Here

COVERED BRIDGE PRESS

North Attleborough, Mass.

FOR

ELEANOR

AND THE

SEA DOG

Printed in the United States of America

ISBN 0-924771-38-0

10 9 8 7 6 5 4 3 2 1

REPUBLICAN CANDIDATES
DEMOCRATIC CANDIDATES
A SHOT IN THE DARK
ONLY INDICTED NEVER CONVICTED
SIX OF ONE HALF DOZEN OF THE OTHER
LESSER OF TWO EVILS
POWER CRAZED BUT HAS ALL HIS OWN TEETH
MACHINE MAN BUT
NOT TOO CORRUPT
WOMANIZER BUT
DON BOUSQUET
AT THE POLLS IN R.I.

EARLY RESIDENT OF JAMESTOWN

BACK TO SCHOOL IN CRANSTON, R.I.

"GOSH, THE STATE HOUSE IS REAL NEAT, MISTER. BUT, WHERE'S BRUCE'S OFFICE?"

" ...SO, ANYWAY, CAPTAIN, I WAS THINKING... JUST UNTIL WE GET THIS FUEL PROBLEM SORTED OUT, COULD YOU, YOU KNOW, MAYBE LIKE EXTINGUISH THAT CIGARETTE ? "

THE HIGH PRICE OF
BOBBING FOR CLAMCAKES

"THIRTY-SIX THOUSAND LAWYERS LIVING IN WASHINGTON, D.C.! THAT EXPLAINS IT. THAT EXPLAINS EVERYTHING!!"

"IT'S NOT TOO BAD, MA ... I
GET A DOLLAR A DAY TO WORK IN
THE LAUNDRY. THAT'S ONLY FOUR
DOLLARS LESS THAN I GOT AS A
MEMBER OF THE GENERAL ASSEMBLY."

ANY RHODE ISLAND CUMBERLAND FARMS
STORE, SEVENTEEN MINUTES AND TWELVE
SECONDS AFTER A FORECAST OF TWO TO
FOUR INCHES OF SNOW

" HENRY, I'M COLD. RUN BACK TO THE CAR AND GET MY SWEATER ! "

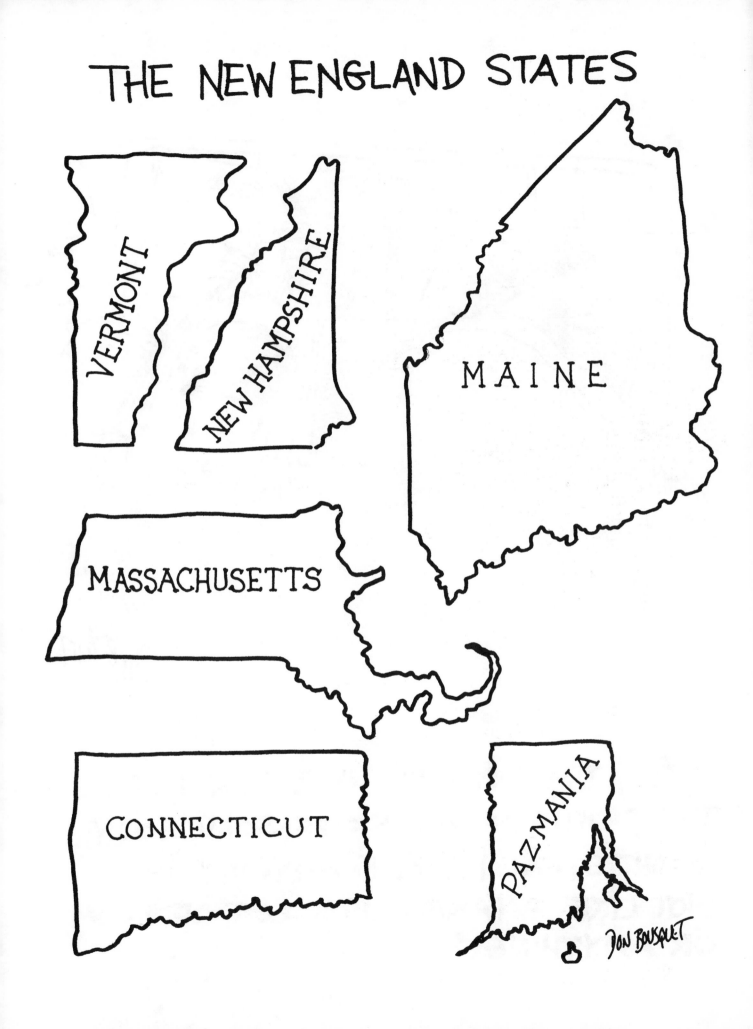

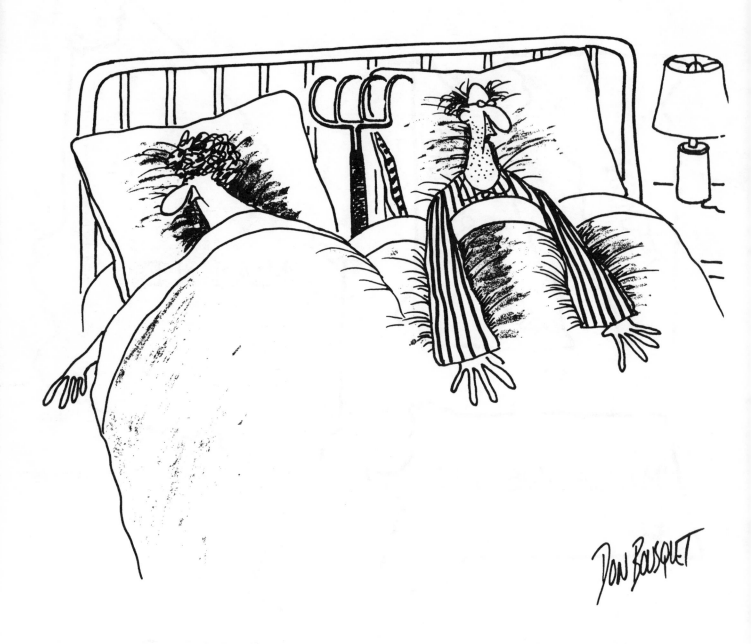

"WELL, I'M SORRY BUT IF I LEAVE IT IN THE PICKUP OR THE SKIFF SOMEBODY MIGHT STEAL IT. AND ANYWAY, IT'S NOT LIKE IT TAKES UP A LOT OF ROOM OR ANYTHING."

BEN AND ARETHA FRANKLIN

"BE CAREFUL, FOR GOD'S SAKE! YOU'RE IN RHODE ISLAND NOW AND YOU COULD CAUSE A VERY SERIOUS ACCIDENT BY ACTUALLY YIELDING AT A YIELD SIGN!!"

" I'M GLAD YOU LIKE IT, SON. I
WHACKED IT TOGETHER FROM OVER
SEVEN THOUSAND OF THOSE FUNNY
BLACK THINGS YOU HAVE TO PEEL OFF
THE NECKS OF STEAMED CLAMS. "

"ALL THE KIDS ARE MAKING THEM.
IT'S A SCALE MODEL OF JOHNSTON."

HEAVY DOODY

A SCENE FROM THE UPCOMING UNIVERSAL STUDIOS RELEASE, 'DANCES WITH QUAHOGS'

"TODAY, CLASS, WE WILL DISCUSS BILLY ECKERT'S REPORT, 'PROVIDENCE ... THE NINETIES OR FESTERING H... THE WAY TO CAPE COD?'"

THE CODFATHER

DON BOUSQUET

" THE FORMER OWNER HAD TWO CHILDREN.
THIS WAS THEIR ROOM... THEY JUST
LOVED TO LOOK AT THE BAY. "

" TREMENDOUS SOURCE OF CALCIUM.
AND TO THINK I'VE BEEN JUST
THROWING AWAY THE SHELLS
FOR YEARS ! "

"ONCE MORE AND ALL TOGETHER NOW...
'I SEEN YOUR LAST FIGHT AT THE CIVIC
CENTER AND YOU WAS AWESOME.'"

" WOOPSY DAISY... "

QUAHOGMAID

WOODROW F. BUONANNO ELEMENTARY

" NOW CHILDREN, IF TEACHER 'A' HAS THREE YEARS TO RETIREMENT AND TEACHER 'B' HAS TWENTY-THREE YEARS TO RETIREMENT, WHICH TEACHER IS THE POOR DEVIL AND BY HOW MANY YEARS ?"

"QUAHOG STINGER, MA'AM...AND IT'S PAID FOR."

THE MIDDLEBRIDGE/VERRAZANO BRIDGE

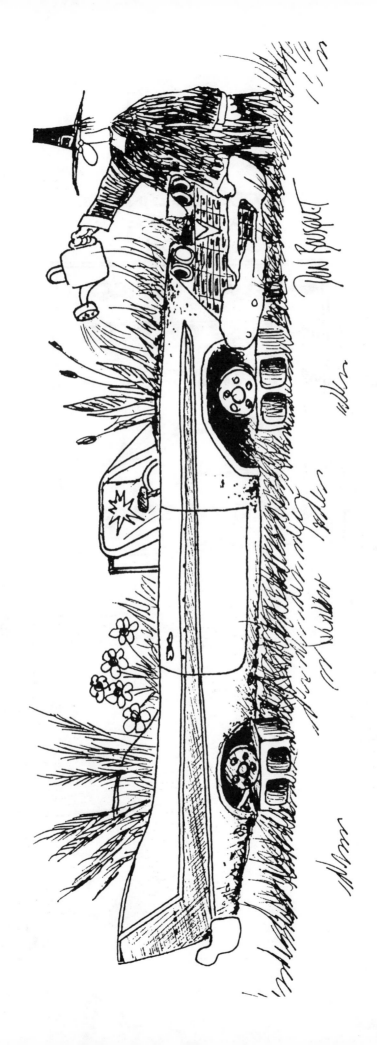

PLYMOUTH PLANTATION

65 MILLION YEARS AGO —
JUST BEFORE THEY WERE WIPED OUT...

FOLLOWING THEIR CONVENTION IN RENO, NEVADA, MEMBERS OF THE RHODE ISLAND SHELLFISHERMAN'S ASSOCIATION ARRIVE AT GREEN AIRPORT.

LITTLE NICKS ON
THE HALF SHELL

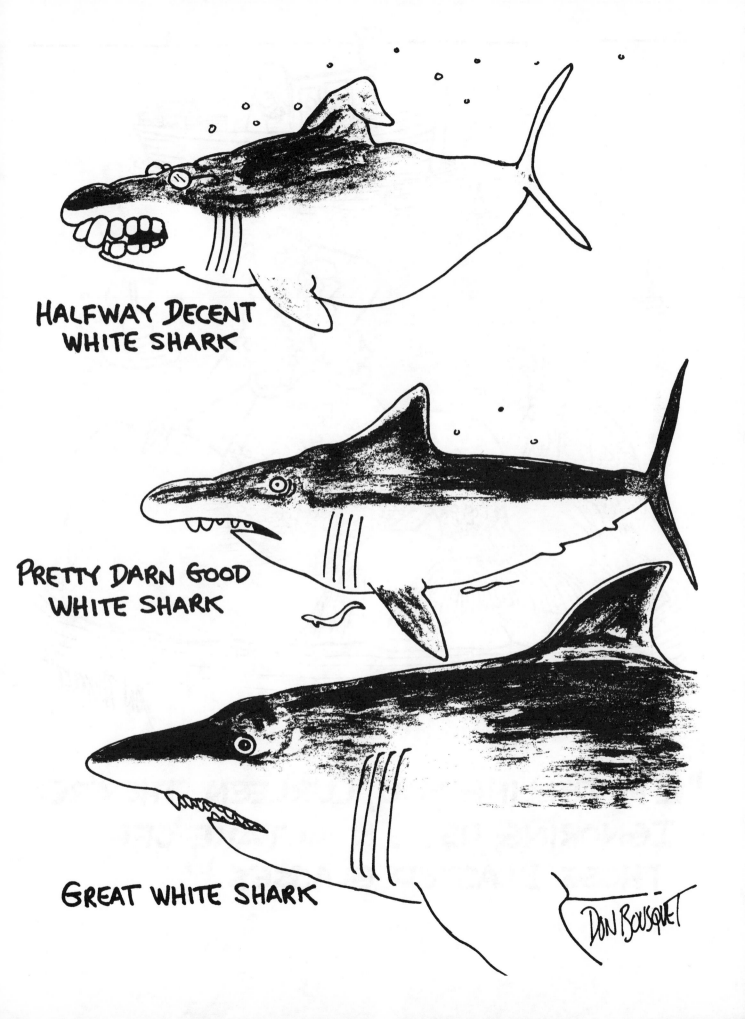

HALFWAY DECENT
WHITE SHARK

PRETTY DARN GOOD
WHITE SHARK

GREAT WHITE SHARK

Don Bousquet

"I'M TELLING YOU, LURLEEN, THEY'RE IGNORING US... NOW TAKE OFF THOSE BLASTED GLASSES!"

CHRISTMAS CODS

RHODE ISLAND POLITICAL CANDIDATE
POSING FOR A CAMPAIGN POSTER

LITTLE RED RHODE ISLAND HOOD

"AND LIKE JUST THEN THIS BIG WOLF COMES UP TO ME, RIGHT? AND HE ASKS ME LIKE WHAT I GOT IN THE BASKET, Y'KNOW? AN' I SAYS I'M BRINGING THIS STUFF TO MY GRANMA, RIGHT? THEN HE LIKE ASKS ME WHAT THE STUFF IS SO I TELL HIM I GOT COFFEE SYRUP AND LITTLE NECKS AND SNAIL SALAD AND JUST THEN THE WOLF HE LIKE SORT OF GAGS AND RUNS OFF INTO THE FOREST WITH HIS TAIL BETWEEN HIS LEGS, Y'KNOW?"

RHODE ISLANDERS IN DRIVING SCHOOL

RHODE ISLANDER IN INTENSIVE CARE

DON BOUSQUET

LARGE MOUSE BASS

TWO DAYS AFTER THE COMPLETION
OF THE NEW JAMESTOWN BRIDGE
THE POLAR ICE CAP MELTS.

PROFESSOR ERNST ZIFF OF THE
BROWN UNIVERSITY ECONOMICS DEPT.
WITH ONE OF THE ACTUAL TUBES
RHODE ISLAND HAS BEEN HEADING
DOWN FOR SEVERAL YEARS

WOMEN & INFANTS HOSPITAL OF RHODE ISLAND, 1948

AMONG THESE SIX BABIES ARE A FUTURE LAWYER, MAYOR, JUDGE, CREDIT-UNION OFFICIAL, LEGISLATOR AND A MEMBER OF ORGANIZED CRIME. TODAY YOU STILL CAN'T TELL THEM APART.

" ISN'T IT AMAZING WHAT A
HAIRDRESSER FROM CRANSTON CAN
DO WITH A LITTLE THINNING HAIR
PROBLEM LIKE MINE ! "

♫ WHY DO BIRDS SUDDENLY APPEEEAR EV'RY TIME YOU ARE NEEEAR ? ♫

GUIDANCE
COUNSELOR

JEEZ, WHAT A
FUNNY DUCK THIS
SALTY BRINE KID IS.

DON BOUSQUET

" WELL, I LIKE TO GET UP REAL
EARLY IN THE MORNING. REAL EARLY.
I MEAN REEEAL EARLY. THEN I LIKE
TO GET REAL CHEERFUL AND WAKE
EVERYBODY UP. MY MOM, MY DAD, THE
NEIGHBORS. IS THERE A JOB LIKE THAT? "

THE REAL REASON THAT UPPER NARRAGANSETT BAY QUAHOGS ARE OFF-LIMITS

"NO, I DON'T KNOW WHAT TIME IT IS. GO ASK THE LIFEGOD."

RISDUCKS

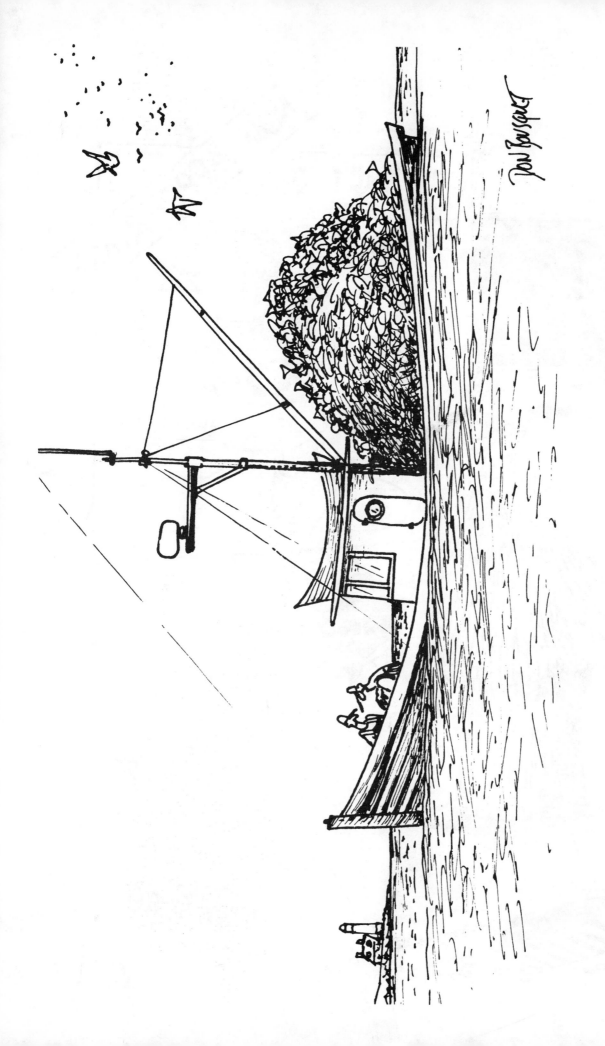

" TAILS.... YOU GET TO CLEAN 'EM. "

"NOW JUST HOLD ON A COTTON PICKIN' MINUTE THERE, BUSTER. I CERTAINLY DON'T BELONG HERE. WHERE I COME FROM I WAS IMPORTANT. I'M A MAN OF POSITION. LISTEN, FELLA, YOU'RE TALKING TO A CREDIT UNION MANAGER."

STOVEHENGE

BUILT LONG AGO BY THE WOOD-
BURNING DRUIDS OF HOPE VALLEY,
RHODE ISLAND

" MISS PARTELO, SEND IN MY RAKE. "

" GOOD EVENING, THIS IS THE SIX O'CLOCK REPORT... HELL FROZE OVER TODAY AND IN A RELATED STORY, THE JAMESTOWN-VERRAZANO BRIDGE WAS COMPLETED AMID MUCH FANFARE BY AREA POLITICIANS... "

A WORLD OF TROUBLE AHEAD

"THE SIGN? SHOOT, I'VE ALWAYS FIGURED IT SAYS, 'FEATHERED FRIENDS LUXURY CONDOMINIUMS'..."

LITTLE COMPTON ROAD SIGN

PROVIDENCE STREET SIGN

DEAR EDNA,

JUST A QUICK NOTE TO KEEP YOU UP TO DATE ON OUR BUS TOUR OF NEW ENGLAND... IT'S SIMPLY LOVELY, YOU KNOW AND SUCH A SURPRISE THE LITTLE TOWN OF JOHNSTON, R.I. TURNED OUT TO BE! THE TOPOGRAPHY IS MOSTLY FLAT WITH SOME ROLLING HILLS AND ONE SINGULARLY MAGNIFICENT MOUNTAIN! IMAGINE OUR DELIGHT TO SEE THOUSANDS OF SEA BIRDS, GULLS, I WOULD THINK, HOVERING OVER THIS BREATHTAKING PEAK SO DISTANT FROM THE OCEAN.

TOMORROW WE MOTOR TO FALL RIVER AND THEN IT'S OFF TO NEW BEDFORD! WHEN!

CORDIALLY, VIVIAN & LEONARD

"OKAY, WHICH ONE OF YOU CLOWNS KEEPS PUTTING THAT THERMOSTAT UP SO HIGH?"

"WE'VE BEEN SPENDING TOO MUCH TIME ON THE BAY AND NOT ENOUGH TIME WITH THE HYGIENIST, HAVEN'T WE?"

NEW SQUID ON THE BLOCK

"BASICALLY, YOUR COMPUTERS TAKE CARE OF MOST OF THE ACTUAL FLYING."

" SO, JUST STOP FEELING SORRY FOR YOURSELF AND START THANKING YOUR LUCKY STARS THAT YOU'RE A RHODE ISLANDER AND THIS IS JUST A POTHOLE IN THE ROAD OF YOUR POLITICAL CAREER."

HANSEL AND GRETEL
IN WEST GREENWICH

FOR SALE :

USED DUMP TRUCK

• ONE PREVIOUS MUNICIPAL OWNER
• LOW MILES
• WELL MAINTAINED
• ROOMY CAB, SLEEPS TWO

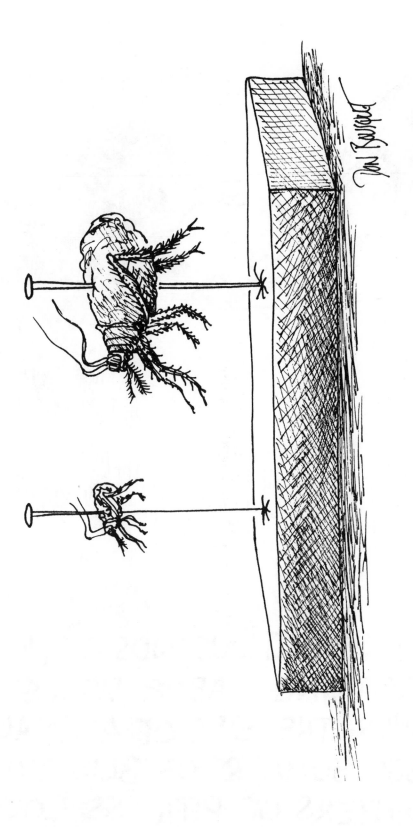

THE LESSER OF TWO WEEVILS (LEFT)

"I SEE... I SEE THOUSANDS OF HOURS OF BACK-BREAKING LABOR WHILE LEANING OVER THE SIDE OF A SMALL BOAT... I SEE SUMMERS OF BLISTERING HEAT AND WINTERS OF PITILESS COLD... I SEE BEER... LOTS OF BEER.... THAT'S ABOUT IT."

WICKFORD, R.I. 50,000 B.C.

MEET FRANK AND EILEEN. HE SUPERVISES
A TEAM OF HIGHWAY MAINTENANCE TRUCK
DRIVERS AND SHE'S A HIGH OFFICIAL AT THE
REGISTRY OF MOTOR VEHICLES.

SUNBELT YANKEES

METAL FATIGUE

" YUP, GOT AS MUCH FOR IT AS I PAID FOR IT BACK IN '72... TRY THAT WITH YOUR MERCEDES BENZ! "

CHEERLEADER, MOLLICONE HIGH

"YO, VITO! Y'KNOW ALL THEM MEETINGS WE'VE HAD ABOUT THE SO-CALLED IMPENDING COLLAPSE OF THE JAMESTOWN BRIDGE?..... WELL, THE NEWPORT BRIDGE JUST CAVED IN."

"LOOK, WE PROBABLY WON'T GET BUSTED FOR KNOCKING OVER THE JEWELRY STORE. BUT IF WE DO GET BUSTED — NO PROBLEM... THE TIME WE SPEND IN THE CAN WILL COUNT TOWARD OUR R.I. STATE PENSIONS."

"I WAS BORN IN PROVIDENCE. NEVERTHELESS, I TEND TO WEAR COLOR-COORDINATED CLOTHES AND AVOID PASSING ON THE RIGHT IN HEAVY TRAFFIC.... I DON'T USE DOUBLE NEGATIVES OR WEAR NECK JEWELRY. I HAVE NEVER ATTENDED A BARRY MANILOW CONCERT AND ENJOY NO CONNECTIONS AT CITY HALL..... DOCTOR, WHAT'S WRONG WITH ME ???"

THE LONE QUAHOGGER, HIS FAITHFUL SIDEKICK, KLAMBOE AND THEIR NEW BOAT WHICH THEY RECENTLY BOUGHT FROM A MAN IN FALL RIVER.

"THIS IS THE LAST TIME YOU'RE DRAGGING ME OUT TO A MOVIE IN CRANSTON!"

COMMERCIAL FISHERMEN

"OH, MY GOODNESS! IT'S THE EIGHTH JOE MOLLICONE WE'VE HAD TONIGHT!"

"... A POLAND SPRING TANKER TRUCK WITH FIFTY-THOUSAND GALLONS OF FRESH WATER ABOARD CRASHED INTO A PAWTUCKET EXXON STATION THIS MORNING CAUSING MASSIVE CONTAMINATION OF THE SUPER UNLEADED TANKS AND ... "

"OF COURSE IT DOESN'T BOTHER YOU TO HAVE TO LIVE ON A TINY PIECE OF LAND IN THE MIDDLE OF NOWHERE WITH NOTHING BUT CLAMS TO EAT... YOU'RE FROM RHODE ISLAND!"

You Can Draw

The Berenstain Bears®

Featuring all your favorite Bear Country friends!

Living Lights™
A Faith Story

by Mike Berenstain

Based on the characters created by
Stan & Jan Berenstain

ZONDERKIDZ

You Can Draw The Berenstain Bears®

Copyright © 2018 by Berenstain Publishing, Inc.
Illustrations © 2018 by Berenstain Publishing, Inc.

Requests for information should be addressed to:

Zonderkidz, 3900 Sparks Drive SE, Grand Rapids, Michigan 49546

ISBN 978-0-310-76220-1

Design: Cindy Davis

Printed in China

18 19 20 21 22 /DSC/ 22 21 20 19 18 17 16 15 14 13 12 11 10 9 8 7 6 5 4 3 2 1

Table of Contents

Let's Get Started!

Before you start drawing, you'll need a few tools. Start with a Number 2 or HB pencil, an eraser, and a pencil sharpener. When you finish your drawing, you'll be adding color using colored pencils, markers, or a brush with watercolor or acrylic paint. You'll need a tray to hold the colors and a container for water to mix with the colors.

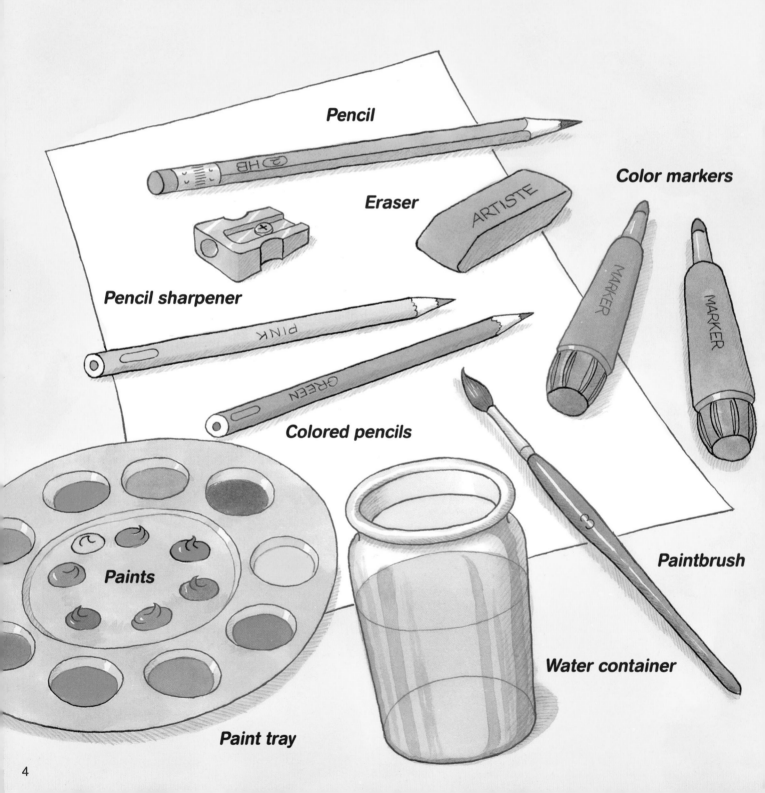

Pencil

Eraser

Color markers

Pencil sharpener

Colored pencils

Paintbrush

Paints

Water container

Paint tray

Tips from Mike

In this book, you'll learn how to draw the Berenstain Bears in a few easy steps. The first half introduces basic drawing steps, while the second half is more advanced and gives you the opportunity to use what you've learned. You'll get tips from Mike Berenstain about drawing the characters all along the way. Soon, you'll be drawing the Berenstain Bears on your own!

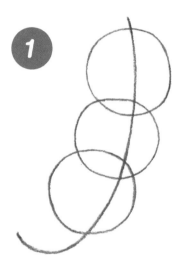

Sketch in the basic shapes, first. Make these lines light so they can easily be erased.

New steps are shown in blue, so you can see what comes next.

Use the blue lines as a guide to draw details.

Make the lines you want to keep darker, erasing the rest.

Finally, add color with crayons, paints, markers, or colored pencils.

The Story of
The Berenstain Bears

At the far edge of Bear Country, Mama Bear, Papa Bear, and Small Bear lived in a cave halfway up Great Bear Mountain. Papa had plenty to do with his woodcutting and furniture making. Mama kept busy managing things and tending the vegetable garden. Small Bear had fun playing with his mountain friends.

But, after a while, the trees for Papa's furniture making grew scarce on the mountainside. And it was getting hard to grow enough vegetables in the rocky soil. So the family decided to move down into the valley. They moved to a big, beautiful tree house down a sunny dirt road deep in Bear Country. The neighbors all welcomed them.

Papa set to work fixing the place up. He added a playroom down in the tree's roots and he made the garage into a shop for his woodwork. They would need room for their growing family.

Before long, Mama had a baby girl cub. They called her Sister and Small Bear now became Brother Bear. At first Sister slept in a crib in Mama and Papa's room. But when she was bigger, Papa built a bunk bed and Brother and Sister shared a room.

A few years later, another baby girl cub came along. She was such a sweet little thing they named her Honey. Now, Papa hollowed out one of the tree's great branches to make Honey a room of her own.

The cubs love their grandparents, Grizzly Gramps and Gran, who live nearby in a house made from the trunks of trees. The cubs always enjoy visiting them. Gran bakes wonderful cookies and Gramps can do magic tricks.

The Bear family has many good neighbors. Farmer Ben and Mrs. Ben live just down the road. It's fun to help out around their farm.

Another good friend is Professor Actual Factual Bear. He's a scientist who runs Bear Country's museum. It's interesting to look at the stars through the professor's telescope.

Brother and Sister go to the Bear Country School where they have many good friends. Brother's best bud is his cousin Fred. Sister's best friend is Lizzy Bruin. Some other friends are Ferdy Factual—Professor Actual Factual's nephew, Too-Tall Grizzly, and Queenie McBear. Too-Tall can be a bit of a handful. And Queenie is a little snooty from time to time. Still, they all get along very well.

The cubs like their teachers, Teacher Jane and Teacher Bob, and they enjoy school activities like sports, school plays, and holiday concerts. The school's principal is Mr. Honeycomb. The cubs think he's a good principal—strict but fair.

The Bear family loves living in Bear Country. It's a beautiful place and there are so many things to do and see. They can go on honey hunts or picnics. In the summer there's camping, hiking, and fishing. In the winter they try sledding, skating, and skiing. Trips into Bear Town are nice for a change. There's some shopping and lunch at the Burger Bear. While in town, they can say hello to their friends, Dr. Gert Grizzly and Mayor Horace J. Honeypot.

On the way back from town, the family stops by the Chapel in the Woods. They say hello to Preacher Brown and Mrs. Brown along with Missus Ursula Bruinsky, the Sunday school teacher.

Back home in their cozy tree house, the family gets dinner ready. As it grows dark, they sit down to their favorite feast—honey baked salmon.

"Yum!" says little Honey Bear.

Sister Bear

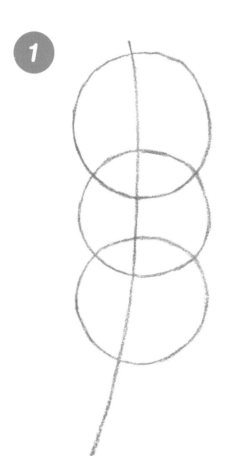

1

Start with three circles—
one for Sister's head,
two for her body.

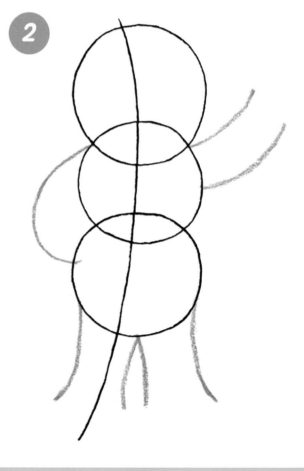

2

Sketch in arms and legs.

3

Use circles, ovals, curves, and straight lines to sketch in shapes of body, face, hands, and feet.

4

Add details.

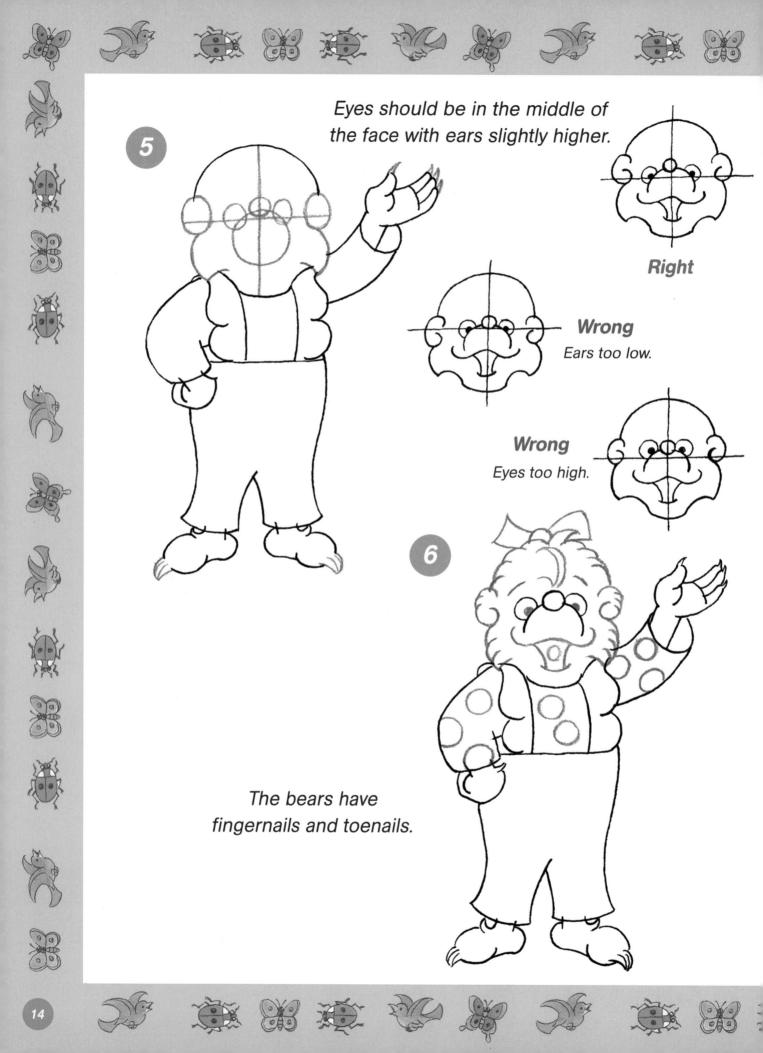

Eyes should be in the middle of the face with ears slightly higher.

5

Right

Wrong
Ears too low.

Wrong
Eyes too high.

6

The bears have fingernails and toenails.

7

An open smiling mouth
is very happy.

A closed smiling mouth
is a little happy.

8

*Use light blue for the shadows
of Sister's white blouse.*

Brother Bear

1

*Brother is running,
leaning forward.*

2

*His arms swing
and his knees bend.*

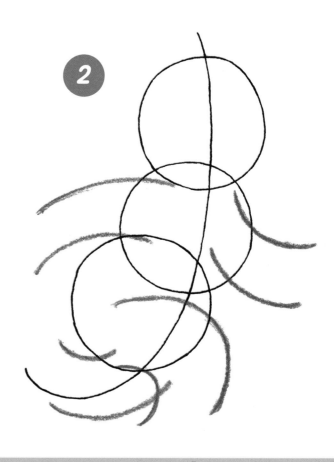

3

His right arm and left leg move back while his left arm and right leg move forward.

Right

Wrong

4

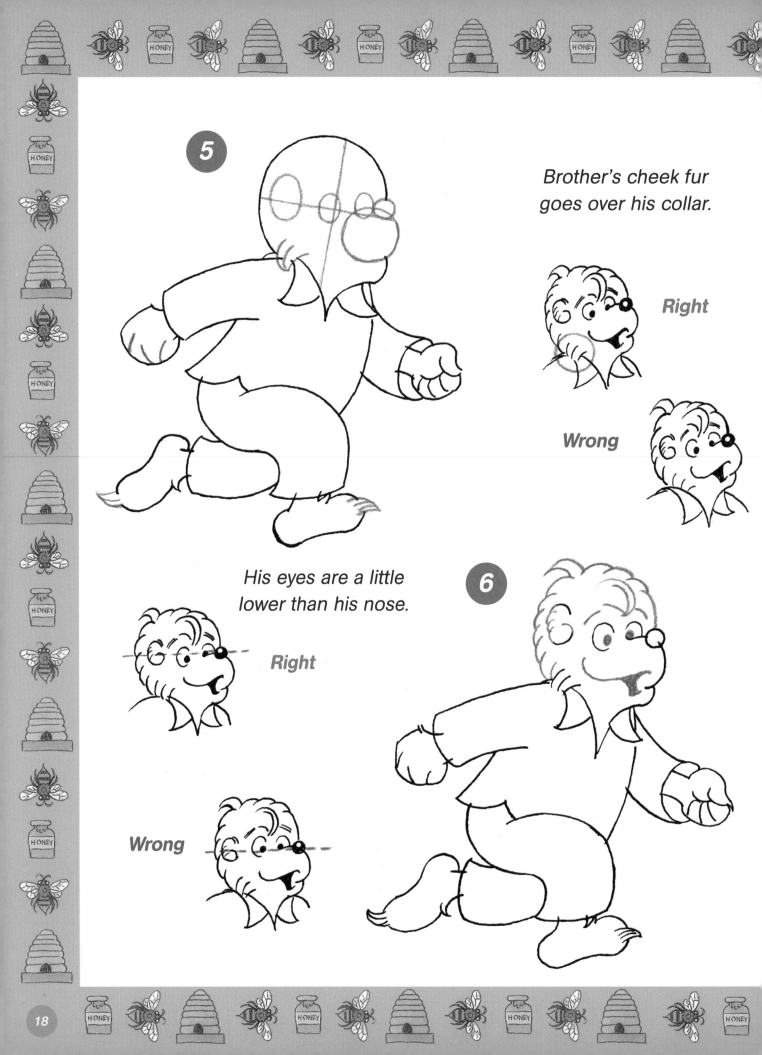

5

Brother's cheek fur goes over his collar.

Right

Wrong

His eyes are a little lower than his nose.

Right

Wrong

6

7

When running, Brother's feet leave the ground. Show this with a shadow.

8

Use light blue for motion lines.

Honey Bear

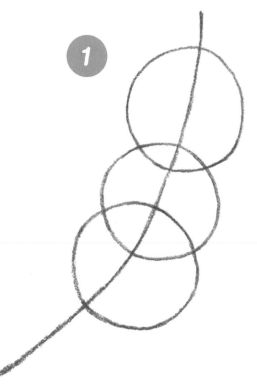

1

*Honey Bear loves to dance—
she sways to one side.*

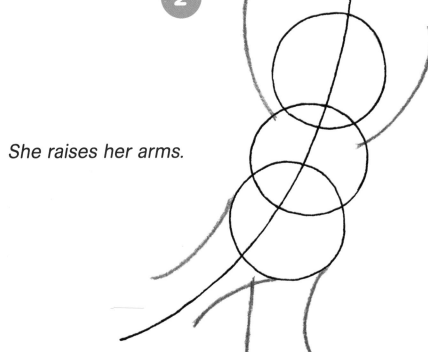

2

She raises her arms.

3

She stands on tiptoe.

4

5

Honey is happy and showing off a little!

The shapes of her eyebrows and mouth show this.

Right

Wrong

6

Honey is so graceful!

Papa Bear

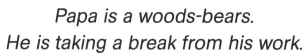

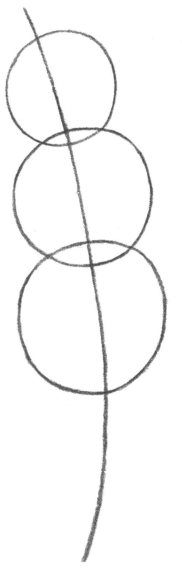

1

Papa is a woods-bears.
He is taking a break from his work.

2

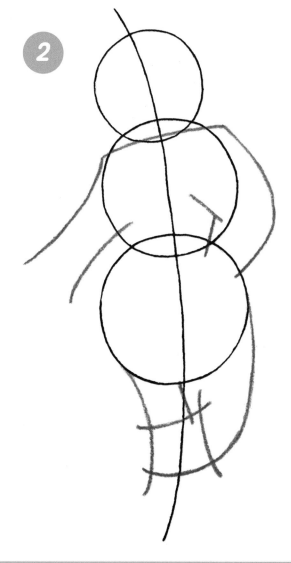

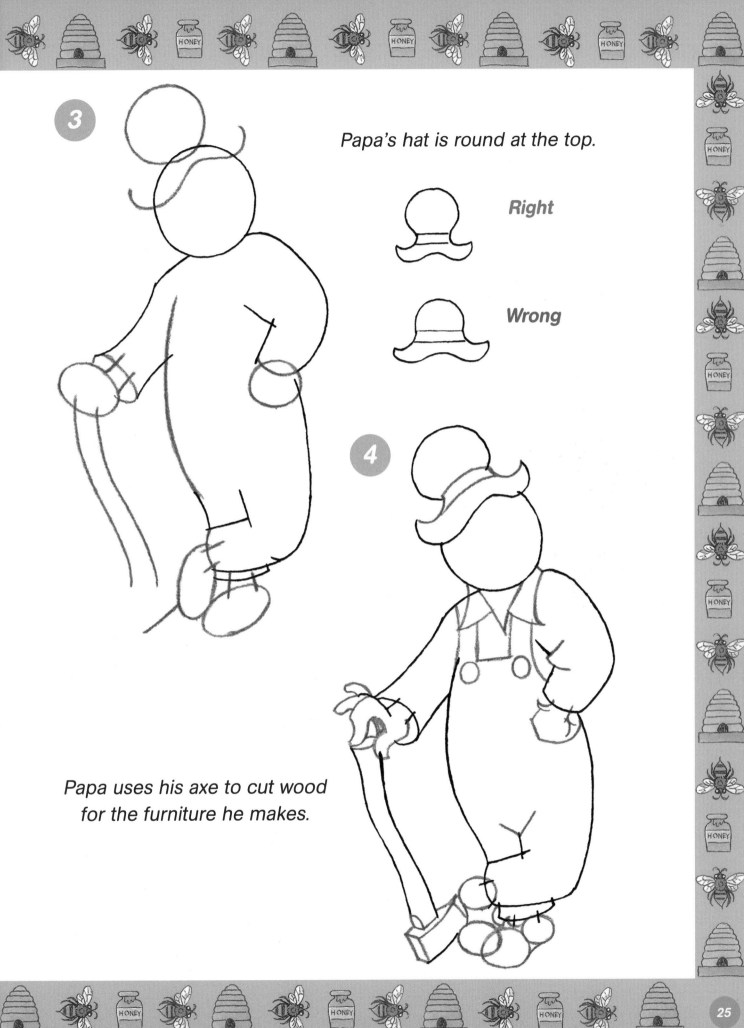

3

Papa's hat is round at the top.

Right

Wrong

4

Papa uses his axe to cut wood
for the furniture he makes.

7

The plaid on Papa's shirt
has three crisscrossed lines.

Right

Wrong

8

Mama Bear

1

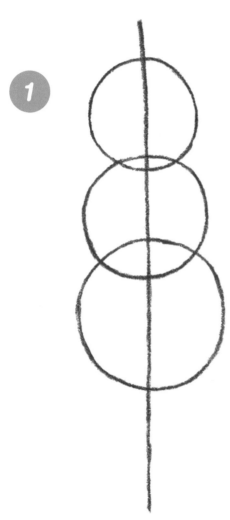

Mama is standing up straight.

2

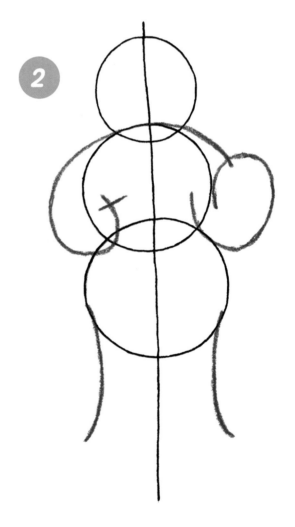

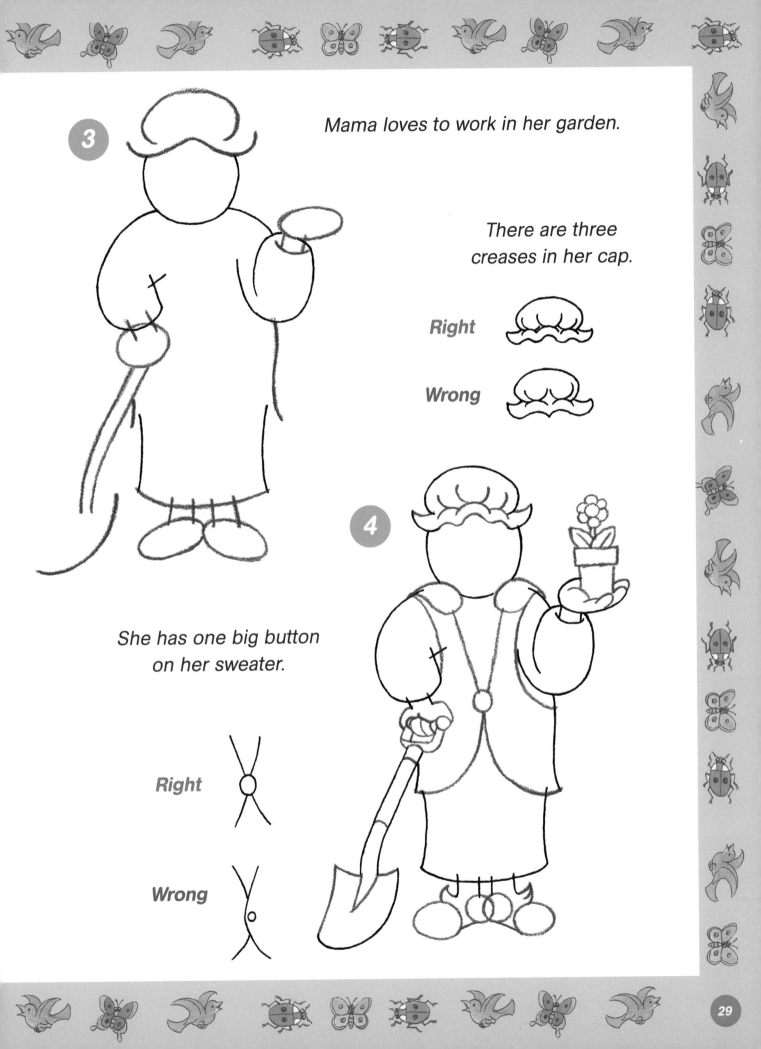

3

Mama loves to work in her garden.

There are three creases in her cap.

Right

Wrong

4

She has one big button on her sweater.

Right

Wrong

29

5

6

The dots on her
dress are large.

Right

Wrong

Grizzly Gramps and Gran

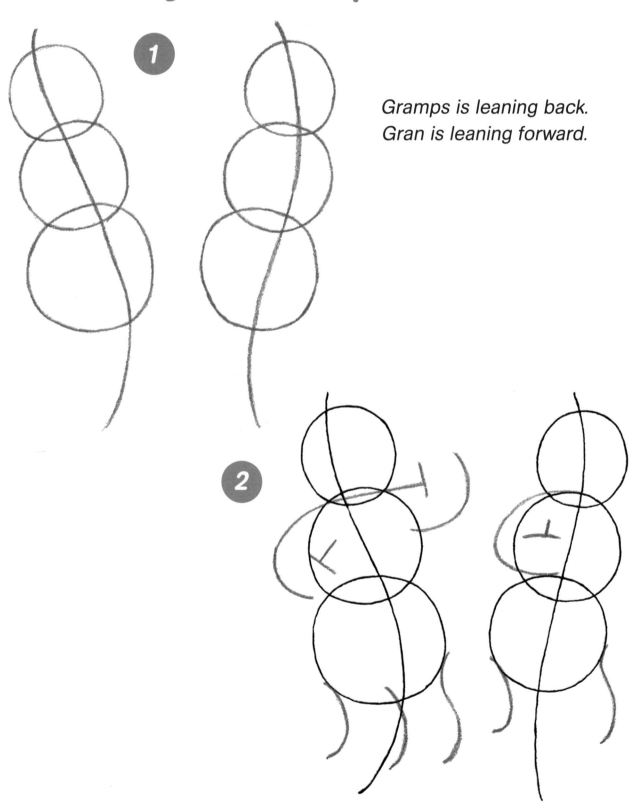

1

Gramps is leaning back.
Gran is leaning forward.

2

Gramps wears a straw hat.
Gran wears a kerchief.

5

Gramps' collar
is unbuttoned.

Right

Wrong

6

Gramps' and Gran's glasses
are square, not round.

Right

Wrong

Farmer Ben and Mrs. Ben

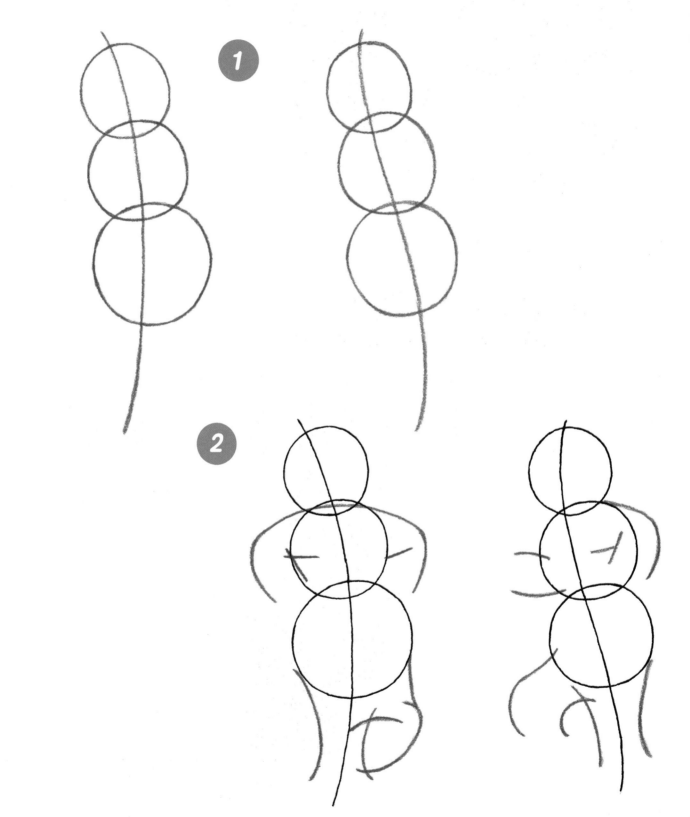

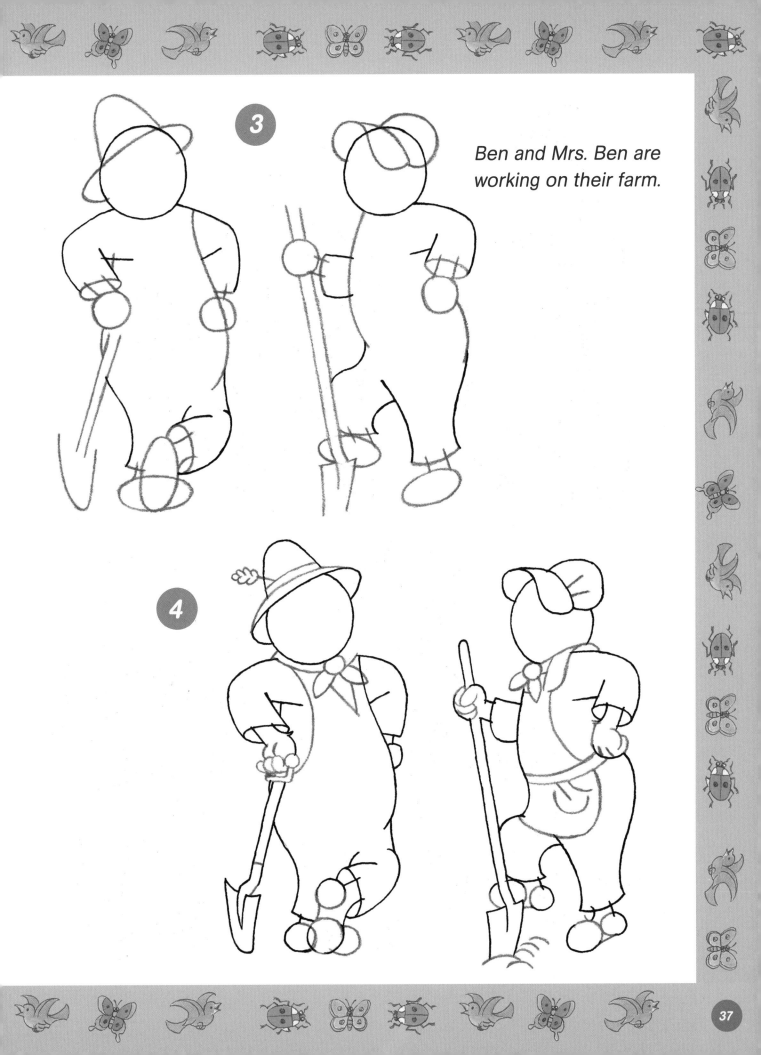

3

Ben and Mrs. Ben are working on their farm.

4

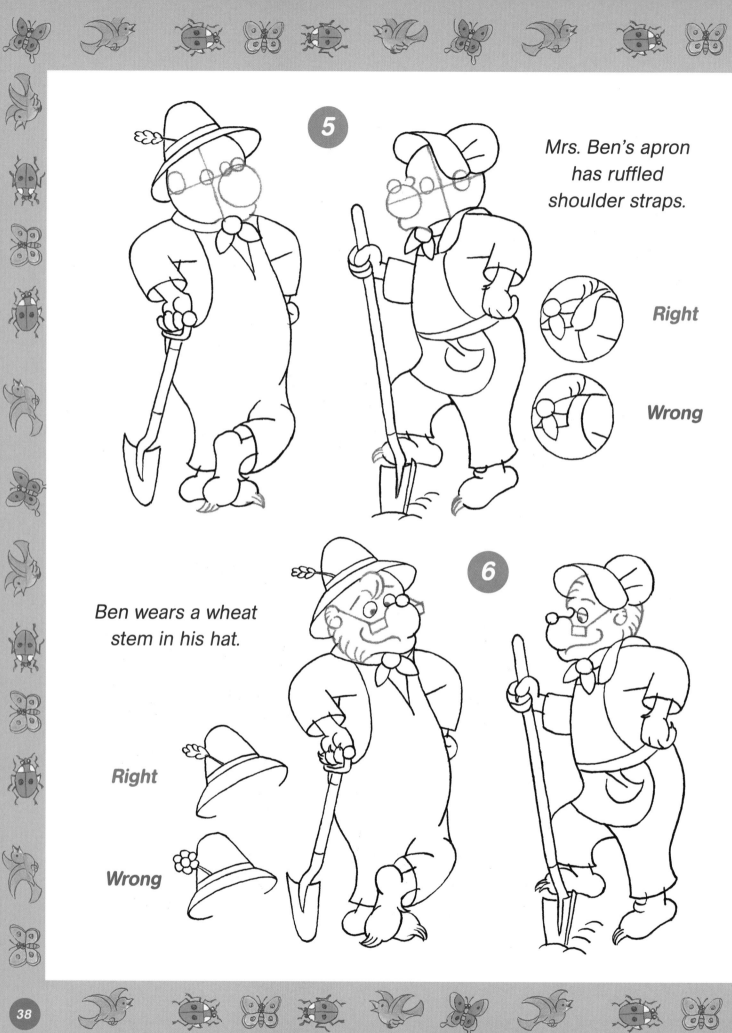

5

Mrs. Ben's apron has ruffled shoulder straps.

Right

Wrong

6

Ben wears a wheat stem in his hat.

Right

Wrong

Professor Actual Factual and Ferdy Factual

1

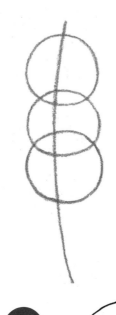

2

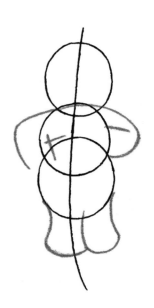

3

The Professor and
Ferdy wear rounded caps.

Right

Wrong

4

They wear short knickers.

Right

Wrong

5

6

The Professor has longer fur.

Right

Wrong

7

8

Lizzy Bruin
and Cousin Fred

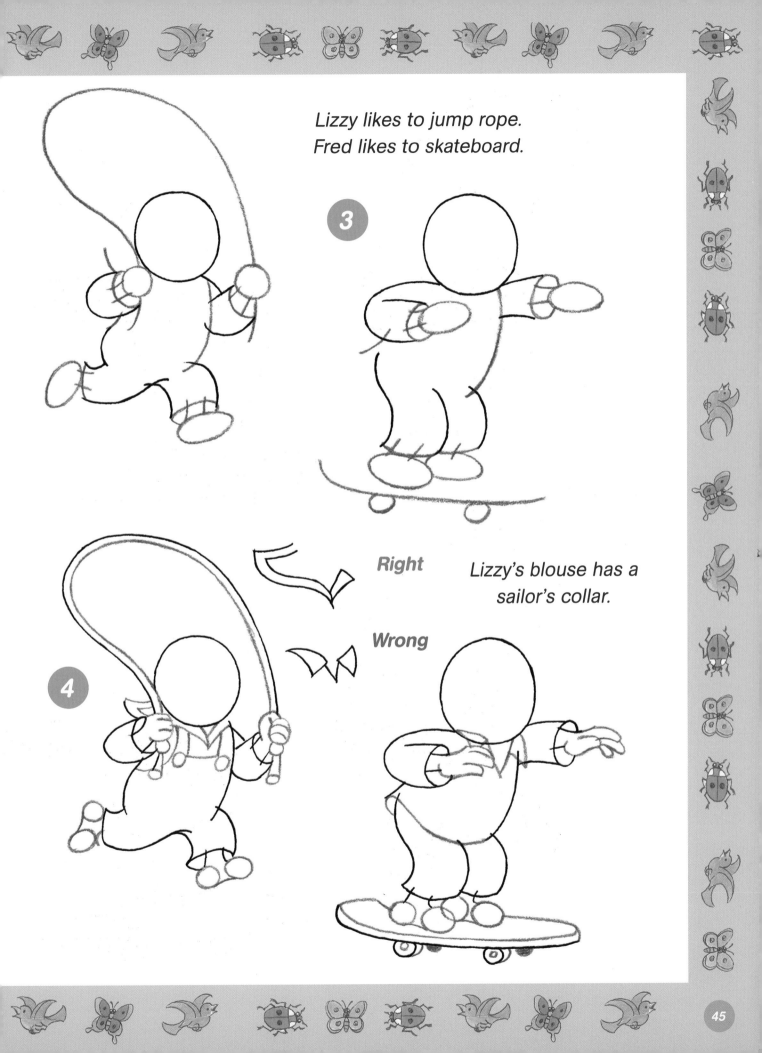

Lizzy likes to jump rope.
Fred likes to skateboard.

3

Right

Wrong

Lizzy's blouse has a
sailor's collar.

4

45

Add motion lines to the jump rope
and skateboard.

Too-Tall Grizzly and Queenie McBear

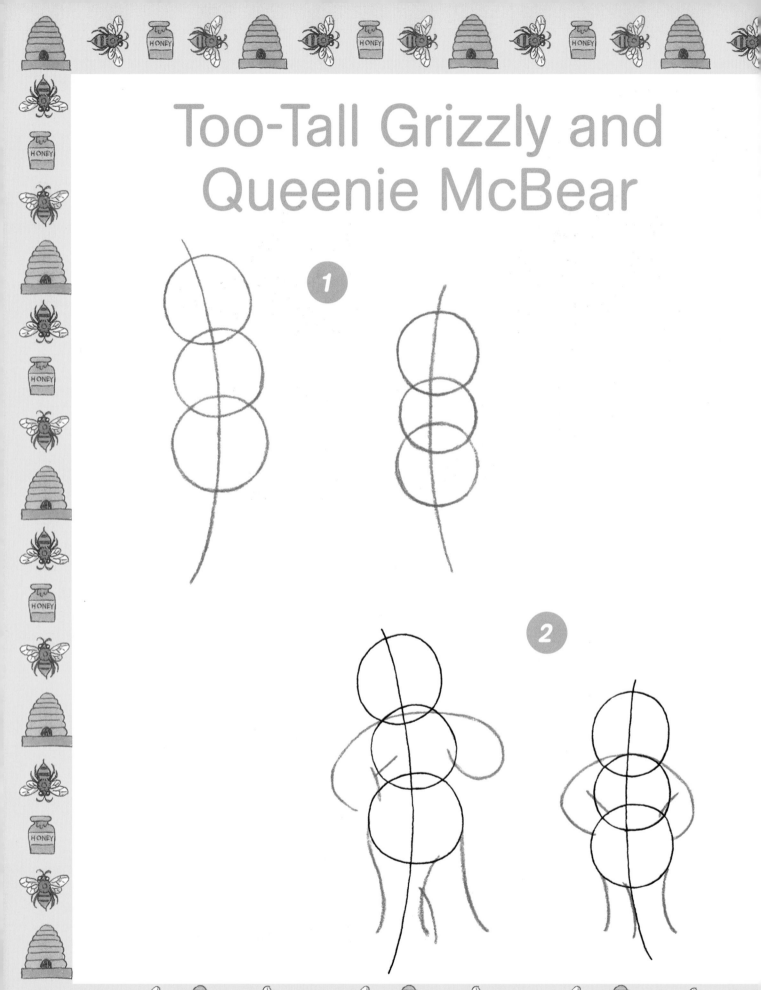

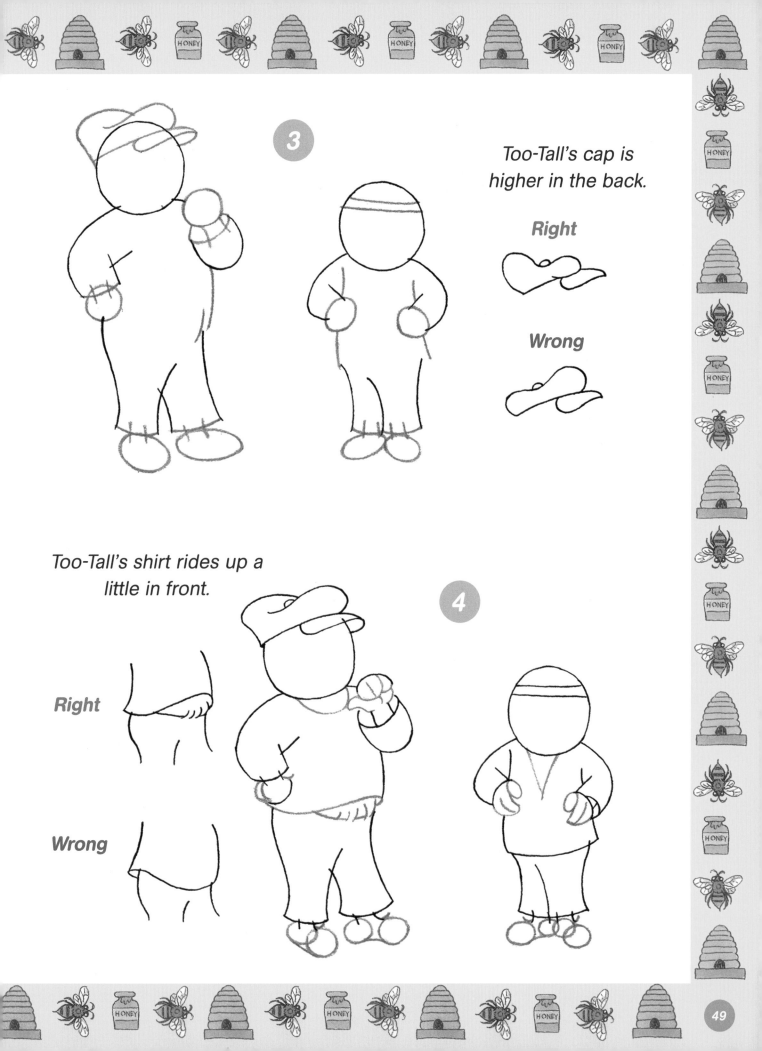

3

Too-Tall's cap is higher in the back.

Right

Wrong

Too-Tall's shirt rides up a little in front.

Right

Wrong

4

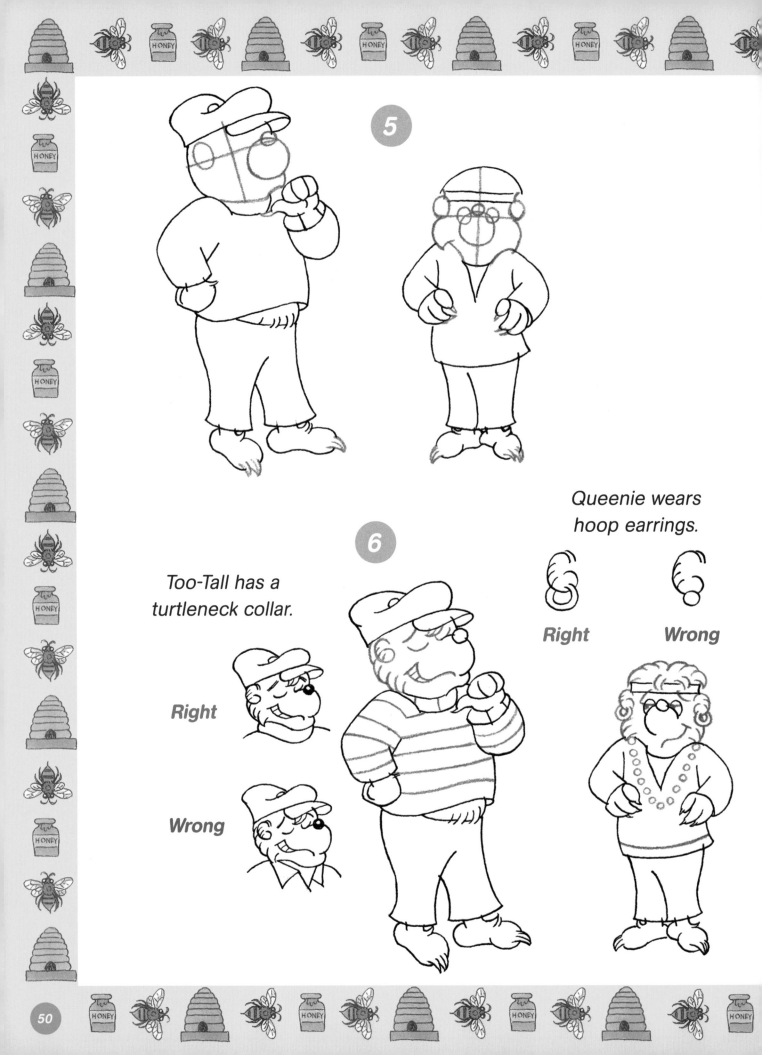

5

6

Queenie wears
hoop earrings.

Right   *Wrong*

Too-Tall has a
turtleneck collar.

Right

Wrong

7

8

Teacher Bob
and Teacher Jane

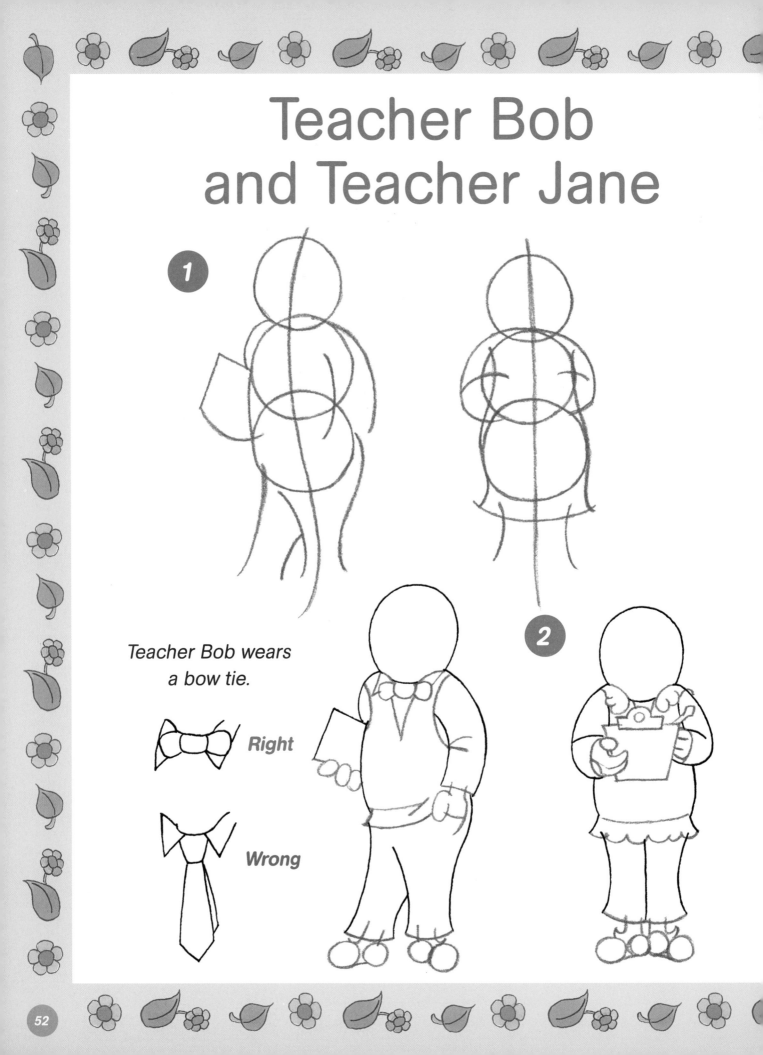

1

2

*Teacher Bob wears
a bow tie.*

Right

Wrong

3

Teacher Jane wears a hair band.

Right

Wrong

4

Principal Honeycomb

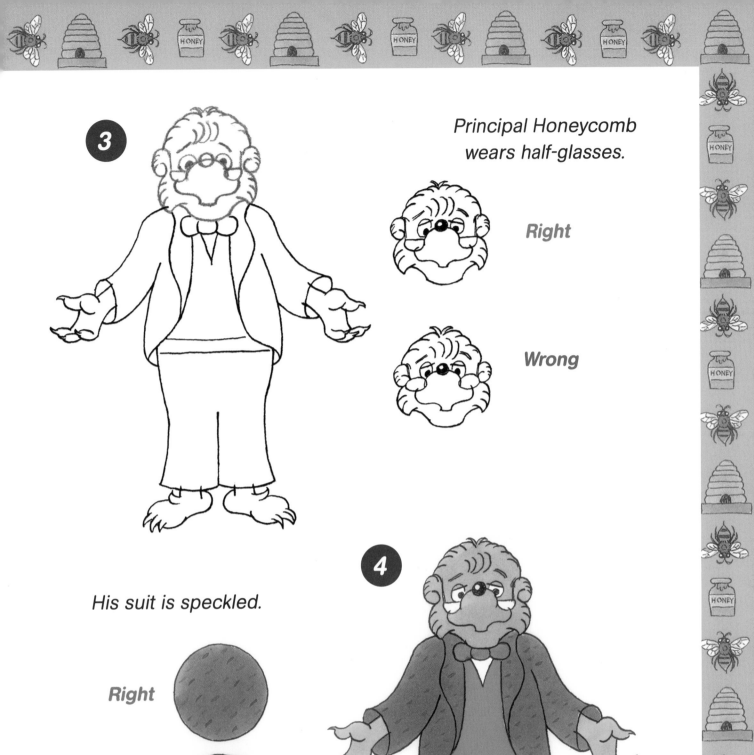

3

Principal Honeycomb wears half-glasses.

Right

Wrong

4

His suit is speckled.

Right

Wrong

Mayor
Horace J. Honeypot

1

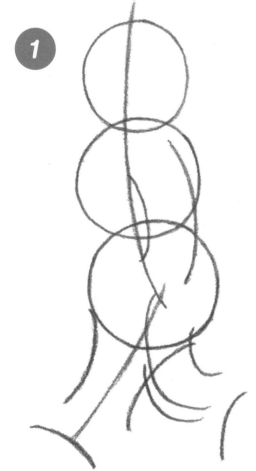

Mr. Mayor's derby hat has a curved-up brim.

Right   **Wrong**

2

3

His glasses have
no ear pieces.

Right   **Wrong**

4

Dr. Gert Grizzly

1

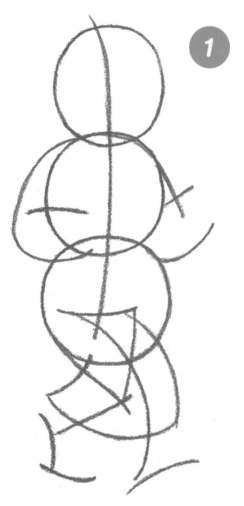

2

3

Dr. Grizzly wears a name tag at the hospital.

 **Right**

 **Wrong**

4

She wears small earrings.

Right

 **Wrong**

Preacher Brown and Mrs. Brown

3

Preacher Brown wears a minister's collar.

Right

Wrong

Right

Wrong

He wears glasses that are straight on top.

4

Missus Ursula Bruinsky

1

2

Missus Ursula's earrings
are pyramid-shaped.

Right

Wrong

Right

Wrong

Her glasses are
attached to a chain.

The End

Now that you've learned how to draw the Berenstain Bears, try creating your own scenes of life in Bear Country. Have fun!